DATE DUE		
OCT 11 1984		
OCT 22 1984	OCT. 29 1992	OC 2 9'00
OCT 2 9 198	OCT. 1 2 1993	OC 2 8'00
OCT 2 5 1985	OCT 19 1993	NO 7 '01
OCT 3 1986	NOV. 8 1993	OC 1 5'02
NOV 8 1986	OCT 2 6 1994	NO 11'02
OCT 14 1987	OCT 25 '95	NO 0 4'08
OCT 28 1987		OC 28 '09
OCT 2 4 1988		OC 2 5 '10
OCT 30 1989	OCT 2 8 '98	
OCT 1 5 1990	OCT 28 '97	
NOV 1 1991	SE 30 '98	

JE

Davis, Maggie S.
Rickety Witch

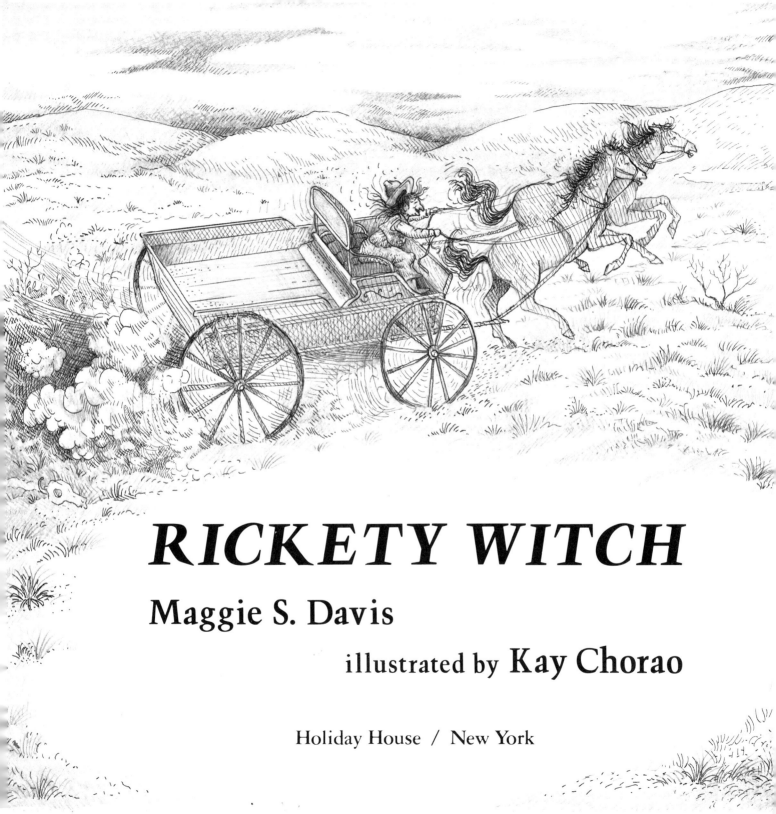

RICKETY WITCH

Maggie S. Davis

illustrated by Kay Chorao

Holiday House / New York

Library of Congress Cataloging in Publication Data

Davis, Maggie S.,
  Rickety witch.

  Summary: A rickety old witch who has been intimidated
for years by two young witches inadvertently gives them
their comeuppance one Halloween.

  [1. Witches—Fiction.   2. Halloween—Fiction]
I. Chorao, Kay, ill. II. Title.
PZ7.D2952Ri 1984   [E]   84-498
ISBN 0-8234-0521-4

Again, for Arnold

IN a cabin on a prairie lived three witches. Two were young but sour as lemon seeds. The third was rickety old but sweet as prairie roses.

One day, outside the cabin door, the witches found a grand
old wagon.

"It's more ours than yours," the sour witches told the sweet
one, and they never, *ever,* let her take the wagon out alone.

But they made her clean it. And they made her polish it. And every day before they took it for a spin, the witches whined and grumbled.

"There's a smudge on the front!"

"There's a smear on the rear!"

"And *you*," they told the rickety witch for no good reason, "are an old fool!"

Well, there wasn't magic strong enough to make the sour witches sweet, so the old witch lived her life the best she could. And one Halloween, while they were climbing on their brooms, the sour witches told her, "Stand guard well 'til we get back, you rickety old fool. We'll boil you in oil if something happens to our wagon."

"Althea Dolores Mathilda McBool may be old, but she's no fool!" the rickety witch sang when they were out of sight. "Rat-a-tat-taggin'! It's *my* turn to use the grand old wagon."

Facing the fading sun to warm her cheekbones, she wheeled away from the hitching post, beyond the climbing roses, past the prairie chickens whirring wildly in the heather, upanddownupanddownupanddown the hills that edged the meadowland, and straight toward town.

"Get your Halloween treats here, children!" she hollered as the wagon careened down Main Street. And that's what the children did.

When Althea stomped twice, the wagon spilled doodads as fit for Halloween as anything seen around for quite some time. There were monster lips and waxen ears, pudgy pumpkin heads, costumes cut from Tyrannosaurus hide, necklaces of bone.

"Here's some icy apple cider," Althea hollered next. But her magic made it pour so fast, some splashed on the horses' bottoms.

Then Althea heard a buzzing sound. "Zinkity-zunk," she wailed. For out, out, out from a nearby tree zigzagged a storm of honeybees.

Althea ducked. The children ran. And the bees swarmed down on the sweet and sticky cider.

"Bzzz," they said and the horses bucked. "BZZZ! BZZZ!" they said and the horses bolted, upanddownupanddown the nearest hills to home. By the time they topped the third hill, they were tuckered.

"Look, my beauties," Althea coaxed, "it's downhill almost all the way from here."

The horses looked. But they wouldn't—*couldn't*—pull the wagon one more inch.

Althea brought them water from a well. She kissed their noses.

"Fiddle-dee-doop," she said. "I've got to get this grand old wagon home." She tickled her toes. She scratched her nose and—what do you know—she thought of something smart.

"No need to fret," she told them. "There's a spell, you see. It's tucked inside my bed."

By then the sky was streaked with black. There was a full moon rising. Althea unhitched the horses and led them home.

"Now where's that spell?" she fussed when she ripped her bed apart and couldn't find it. "Biddle-dee-bump. I can't remember. My brain's as rusty as an old nail."

With the horses for company, Althea rocked and worried on the old front porch. "What will I do," she shivered, "if the witches come home and there's no wagon?"

She stared at it perched high on the distant hill. Then her eyes popped wide. Her teeth did dances on her tongue.

"I'm done for now," she moaned, for flying low around the hill were the sour witches heading dead for home.

Well, it was fortunate that something lucky happened.

The horse to the right of Althea made a sleepy sound. The horse to the left made one, too. And both sounds, mumble-jumbled together, were precisely the words of the magic spell she'd lost.

"Lumma. Mumma. Noomy-ziz," were the mumble-jumble words. Saying them, Althea waved the stick gently, then pointed it over the sour witches' heads toward the wagon on the hilltop.

Instantly, a breeze swirled out from the stick, across the
prairie, up to the hill and behind the wagon. In another instant,
the wagon began to roll.

The sour witches weren't aware of what was happening behind them.

"Where's the wagon?" they screeched, charging toward Althea. "Whoo! Whoo! Whoo! It's the oil for you, old fool!"

The wagon was swallowing every inch of space behind those witches. Down the hill that edged the meadowland it raced, past the prairie chickens whirring wildly in the heather, beyond the climbing roses.

And though Althea called, "Watch out!," it whacked those witches moons away.

"I may be old, but I'm no fool!" Althea sang, sorry for the sour pair but pleased that they were gone. And, swinging her stick, she whirled up a wind to stop the wagon at her door.

From that day to this, Althea has been singing merrier songs. Each morning she hugs the horses. Late at night she rubs their backs. And every Halloween when she delivers all her treats, the wagon comes home safely . . .

whether Althea is driving it . . . or not.